Best Dinosaur Ever

Written by

Lori Rotter

Illustrated by

Vaughan Duck

LFR Creative, LLC

Text & Illustrations copyright © 2023 by Lori Rotter

ISBN Paperback: 979-8-9887529-0-5
ISBN Hardback: 979-8-9887529-1-2

Illustrations and design by Vaughan Duck
www.vaughanduck.com

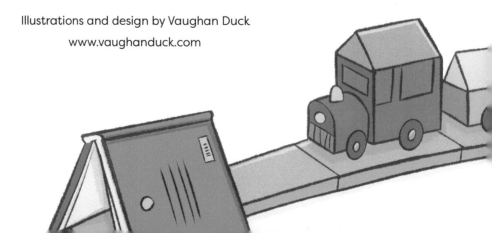

Dedication

To my family for their inspiration, love, and support.

Lori

To all the little dinosaurs in my life. RAWWRR!

Vaughan

Milo flipped through the pages so Daddy could see.

"If I were a dino, what kind would I be?"

"Milo," said Dad, "not to steal all your joy,

But you can't be a dinosaur, you're just a boy!"

Milo pointed to dinos with very large claws,

With razor-sharp teeth inside mighty big jaws.

He wiggled his tooth and looked down at his nose,

"My teeth are not sharp ... and for claws, I have toes."

"Dad, maybe you're wrong. I am funny and clever.

Maybe I am the best dinosaur ever!"

So early next morning, while under the covers,

Milo practiced his roaring, not waking the others.

"I think that I'm ready!" He opened the door,

sneaking up on his sister, he let out a...

Shouted Lulu, "just look at my hair!

What are you doing? You gave me a scare!"

"I'm a

SNEAKY-A-SAURUS!

I'm quiet and rare!

I **sneak** up behind you and give you a **scare**!"

"**Milo**," glared Lulu,

"that's not fair at all.

You have such a **big** roar for someone so small!"

Milo ran to the kitchen, not missing a beat.

I'm a dino who's hungry, so dinos must eat!

"Dinosaurs **CRUNCH!** And they **MUNCH!** Just like me.

I'm the best

CHOMP-A-SAURUS

a 'saurus can be!"

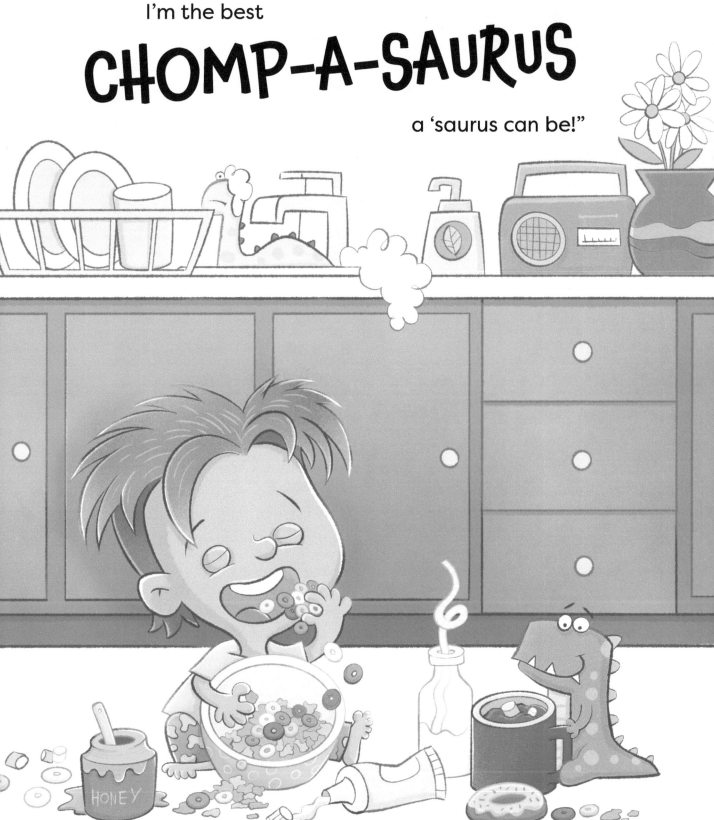

"What's going on?" Mom asked, looking confused.

"My kitchen's a mess! Milo, I'm not amused."

Milo skipped past his Dad with a spring in his step.

"Today I will be the best dinosaur yet!"

"I've snuck up on Lulu with my loud, sneaky roar,

And I crunched, and I munched,

leaving crumbs on the floor."

Then he lined up his dinos in order to see,

deciding what color of dino to be.

Dad said to Milo, "does that make you wild?

You don't look like a dino, you look like a child."

Milo looked at his feet.

His small toes were not claws.

His teeth were not sharp inside mighty big jaws.

Milo called to the kitchen,

"I have some great news!

There's a new kind of dino!

I'll give you some clues."

They were laughing at Milo and rolling their eyes.

"And is this 'new dino' about Milo's size?

Does he **sneak** up and **scare** with a loud, dino **roar**?

Does he **crunch** and he **munch** leaving crumbs on the floor?"

"Yes!" Milo beamed. "He's a new species, I bet.

And he wants to become the best dinosaur yet!"

Dad signaled to Milo. "Come out, let us see!

The best dinosaurus a 'saurus can be!"

Milo rounded the corner and opened the door.

He **stomped** his small feet.

He was **shaking** the floor!

Dressed in his costume with very large claws,

Milo growled,

"RAWWRR!"

inside mighty big jaws.

"You guys were wrong!

I am funny and clever.

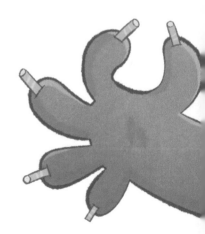

I'm a
MILO-A-SAURUS!

Best dinosaur ever!"

What kind of 'saurus would you be?

Draw your dinosaur costume here.

Lori Rotter

Lori is an award-winning toy designer and debut picture book author.

Her large extended family keeps her laughing and inspires her story and toy ideas. Like in her toys, Lori enjoys sparking the imagination and adding small details for kids to discover.

Lori lives in New York with her husband, lots of fish, and two silly French bulldogs.

Vaughan Duck

Vaughan loves drawing pictures that make kids giggle. He lives downunder in Australia where it's always sunny.

You can visit Vaughan at vaughanduck.com